Black Beauty

Anna Sewell

Adapted by
Mary Sebag-Montefiore

Illustrated by
Alan Marks

Reading Consultant: Alison Kelly
Roehampton University

Contents

Chapter 1

In the beginning

When I was very young my life was gloriously happy. I galloped with other colts by day and slept by my mother's side at night.

But when I was four years old, a
man named Squire Gordon came to
talk to my master, the horse breeder.
He stroked my black coat and
the white star on my forehead.
"Beautiful!" he exclaimed. "Break
him in and I'll buy him!"

Then he touched the white patch on my back. "It's like a beauty spot," he said. "I'll call him Black Beauty."

I shook with fear. I was going to be sold! Would I have to leave my mother? And what was *breaking in*?

"You must learn to wear a saddle and bridle," my mother explained. Then the groom thrust a cold steel bar into my mouth and held it there, with straps over my head and under my throat. There was no escape.

At first the bar frightened me, but with kind words and treats of oats I learned to get used to it.

Just before I was taken to Squire Gordon, my mother spoke to me for the last time. "Now, Black Beauty," she whispered, "be brave. All young horses must leave their mothers to make their way in the world.

Just remember – never bite or rear or kick. And whatever happens, always do your best."

When Squire Gordon's groom
arrived, he jumped on my back and
we rode away. I cantered through
twisting villages until we
reached a long drive.
Apple orchards
stretched out on
either side.

The groom led me into a large,
airy stable with plenty of corn and
hay. A friendly whinny from the
next stall made me look up.

A fat little pony with a thick mane and tail was poking his head over the rail. "I'm Merrylegs," he said. "Welcome to Birtwick Park.

That was John who rode you here," Merrylegs went on. "He's the best groom around – and Squire Gordon is the best owner a horse could have. You'll be happy here."

A tall chestnut mare glared at Merrylegs. "Trouble is, no one knows how long a good home will last," she snapped. "I've had more homes than you've had hot oats."

"Meet Ginger," said Merrylegs. "She bites. That's why she keeps getting sold, even though she's so handsome."

Angrily, Ginger tore at wisps of hay in her manger. "You don't know anything," she muttered. "If you'd been through what I have, you'd bite too."

"Poor Ginger!" I thought. "What could have made her so unhappy?"

Chapter 2

Ginger's story

Over the next few days, John took
me out. At first we went slowly...
then we trotted and cantered,
and ended up in a wonderful
speedy gallop.

"Well, John, how is my new horse?" asked Squire Gordon.

"First rate, Sir," replied John, grooming me carefully. "Black Beauty's as swift as a deer, as gentle as a dove and as safe as houses."

"A lady's horse, perhaps?" asked
the Squire's wife, feeding me pieces
of apple.

"Oh yes, Mrs. Gordon. He'll be a
good carriage horse too. We could
try him out with Ginger," John
suggested.

So I was paired up with Ginger to pull the carriage. During our journeys, she told me the story of her life.

"If I'd had your upbringing, I might be good tempered like you," she began. "My first memory is of a stone being thrown at me."

"Poor you!" I said, but Ginger hadn't finished. "When my first owner broke me in, he shoved a painful bit in my mouth," she went on.

Do as I say!

"I reared up in pain and he fought me with his whip until blood poured from my flanks...

...and then he cut off my tail."

"Why?" I cried. I'd noticed Ginger had no tail, but thought she must have lost it in an accident.

Delightful!

"Fashion," Ginger replied bitterly. "Some people think horses look better with a stump. Now I have nothing to whisk flies away with."

She sighed. "It's agony when they crawl on me and sting."

"Horrible!" I snorted.

"That's not all. My first owner sold me to a rich London gentleman who put me in a bearing rein."

"A what?" I asked.

"It's a tight rein that pulls your neck all the way back. Imagine your tongue pinched, your jaw jerked upright and your neck on fire with pain.

Everyone thought I looked wonderful, but oh, how it hurt! Kindness wins us, not painful whips," said Ginger.

"But we're lucky here," she said, at last. "Squire Gordon hates bearing reins, and John is teaching young Joe, our new groom, to be just as good as he is.

And I'm *trying* to behave now, because everyone's so kind."

Chapter 3

Horses know best

Soon after this, Mrs. Gordon fell ill. We didn't see her for weeks. Then one stormy night John rushed to the stables.

"Best foot forward, Beauty," he cried. "We must ride as hard as we can to fetch the doctor. Mrs. Gordon is at death's door."

We galloped into lashing rain, while thunder and lightning raged around us.

Leaves and twigs danced in the air, torn from their branches by a savage wind.

As we got to the main road, a terrible splitting sound crashed through the darkness. A huge tree had fallen in our path.

23

Gathering all my strength, I
jumped – and sailed over it.

At last we reached the bridge.
I could hear the river roaring.
But the moment I stepped onto
the bridge, I stopped.

"Come on, Beauty," John urged. I couldn't move. I could tell something was wrong. John gave me a light touch of the whip, but I stayed like a statue.

Just then, the moon lit up the bridge. We saw the far end had collapsed into matchsticks, tossing in the raging water.

"Well done, Beauty!" John cried. "We would have been killed. But I'm afraid it's ten miles to the next bridge. We'll have to hurry."

You understand me, don't you Black Beauty?

"Gallop and get there…" I murmured to myself. "Gallop and get there…" The faster I said it, the faster I went.

I raced home with both John and the doctor on my back. I'd never been so tired in my life.

"You're steaming like a kettle," said young Joe. "You're too hot for your blanket. Here, have some ice-cold water."

All through the night I shivered
and sweated and longed for John
to come. When he arrived, he was
horrified. "Joe! You've nearly killed
Beauty!" he shouted. "He's caught
a bad chill.

You should have put on his
blanket – and that icy drink did
him no good at all."

"I didn't know," Joe muttered sulkily.

"Didn't know?" yelled John. "You should make it your business to know. If you don't know, ask!"

"I'm sorry," wept Joe. "I didn't mean to hurt him."

With careful nursing, I recovered, but Joe never forgot the lesson he had learned.

Chapter 4

A terrible time

Mrs. Gordon got better too, but the doctor said she must live in the sun to be really well.

Goodbye Ginger.

Everything was to be sold –
Birtwick Park, Merrylegs, Ginger
and me. Merrylegs went to
the priest.

We said goodbye under the apple
trees, where we'd talked and
played so happily. I never saw
Merrylegs again.

Ginger and I were sold to Lord and Lady Richmore. John had tears in his eyes when he handed us over to Reuben, our new groom.

Look after that temper, Ginger!

Next day, Lord and Lady
Richmore came to inspect us.

"They look very nice, Reuben,"
announced Lady Richmore. "They
can pull my carriage. But you
must put their heads up. High."

"Squire Gordon never used a bearing rein," Lord Richmore reminded her.

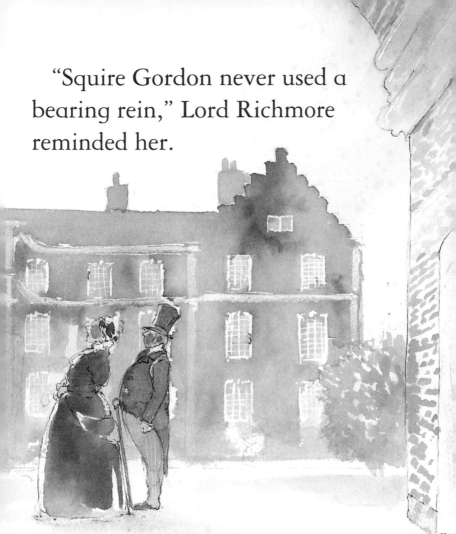

"Well, I won't have horrible, common-looking horses," snapped Lady Richmore.

Reuben pulled my head back and fixed the rein tight. I felt red-hot pain. Ginger tried to jerk her head away, but Reuben forced her rein like mine.

This is agony!

Instantly, I saw why Ginger hated it. I couldn't put my head down to take the strain of pulling the carriage. As the strength drained out of us, Reuben whipped us on.

At last, we came to a grand courtyard crammed with horses and carriages. Ginger couldn't take it any more.

With a wild neigh she reared up, scaring all the horses who crashed into each other, kicking madly. Our carriage toppled over and broke to pieces.

Lady Richmore tumbled out,
unharmed but furious.

Ginger was taken away forever.
I longed to know what happened
to her, but no one mentioned her
name again.

I didn't trust Reuben. He oozed politeness to the Richmores, but secretly he drank too much.

One evening, he took me out for a ride on a road made of fresh-laid sharp stones. My shoe was loose, but Reuben was too drunk to notice.

He never heard the clatter of my
shoe falling off. I don't think he
even noticed me limping. My hoof
split and – I couldn't help it! I fell
onto my knees. Reuben shot to the
ground, hit his head on the cobbles
and lay there, not moving.

I stayed with Reuben all through
the night. When morning dawned,
a group of early walkers came by.
They were shocked at the sight of us.

"That's Reuben," they shouted. "Dead, poor bloke. Thrown by that horse! Vicious brute! That'll be the end of him."

No one knew what really happened. And what would they do to me now?

Chapter 5

Life is a puzzle

"I'm going to sell that bad-tempered Black Beauty to any fool who wants him," Lord Richmore announced.

I was sorry for Reuben, but I couldn't help being thrilled to be leaving Lord and Lady Richmore.

43

I was put into a horse sale.
Buyers prodded me and stared at
me, but no one wanted me.

"Isn't he ugly with those nasty
knees?" I heard someone say.

And he's got a
bad temper.

Finally a kind-looking man paid
a small sum of money for me and
took me away.

The man's name was Jerry
Barker and he lived in London with
his wife and children – Harry and
the twins, Polly and Molly.

"I want you to be my cab horse,"
Jerry told me. "I'll call you Jack."

It was strange to have a new name. My job was to be harnessed to Jerry's carriage, which he called his cab, and pick up passengers when they hailed us in the street.

We worked hard, out all day in all weather – rain, sleet, snow and ice – with hardly any rest.

I didn't mind anything because Jerry was such a kind, honest man. I wanted to do my best for him.

He made sure I was always comfortable and had plenty of food. He never whipped me to go faster, even if customers in a hurry bribed him with extra cash.

"You'll never be rich!" the other cab drivers jeered.

"I have enough, thanks," Jerry replied. "It's not fair on Jack to make him hurry all the time."

Other cab horses weren't so lucky. I often saw them exhausted and miserable, made old before their time with too much work.

Once I saw an old, worn-out chestnut, with a thin neck and bones that stuck out through a badly-kept coat. Its eyes had a dull, hopeless look.

I was wondering why the horse looked faintly familiar when I heard a whisper.

"Black Beauty, is that you?"

It was Ginger! Her beautiful
looks had completely vanished.

She told me she belonged to a
cruel driver who whipped her,
starved her and overworked her.

"You used to stand up for yourself if people were mean to you," I said.

"Yes, I did once, but now I'm too tired," she replied. "I just wish I could die."

"No, Ginger!" I cried. "Keep going! Better times will come."

"I hope they do for you, Black Beauty," she whispered. "Goodbye and good luck."

Soon after that meeting I saw a cart carrying a dead chestnut horse. It was a dreadful sight.

I think it was Ginger. I almost hope it was, for that meant her suffering was over.

Chapter 6

An unexpected ending

One day, a customer of Jerry's made him an offer he couldn't refuse. She asked him to be her groom at her house in the country.

"There's a little cottage for you
and your family," she said. "I wish
I could take Jack too, but I
already have a horse."

"Sorry, old Jack," Jerry
comforted me. "I hope someone
kind will buy you."

But my new master was a cruel man. I had to pull his carts loaded with sacks of corn, and if I was too slow, he whipped me hard. He hardly fed me either, which made me weak.

In the end I simply collapsed in the street. "Stupid horse!" my master grunted. "Is he dead? What a waste of money."

I couldn't move. As I lay there barely breathing, someone came up and poured water down my throat. A gentle voice said, "He's not dead, only exhausted."

Take him. He's no use to me.

The gentle voice belonged to a
horse doctor. I couldn't believe my
luck! The doctor helped me to my
feet, and led me to his stables,
where he gave me a warm mash.

"I think you were a good horse
once," said the doctor, "though
you're a poor, broken-down old
thing now. I'm going to feed you
up and find you a nice home."

Rest, good food and gentle
exercise worked on me like magic.
But when the doctor said I was
ready to leave him, I trembled all
over. I dreaded to think what my
next home would be like.

The doctor took me to a pretty house in a small village. It had a pasture and a comfortable stable, and belonged to two grown-up sisters, Claire and Elspeth Lyefield.

"I'm sure we'll like you," they said, patting me. "You have such a gentle face." I nuzzled them, but I wasn't sure I could trust them.

Their groom led me to the stable and began to clean me. "That white star is just like Black Beauty's," he said, "and the glossy black coat. He's about the same height too. I wonder where Black Beauty is now?"

Soon he came to the tiny knot of white hair on my back. "That's what Squire Gordon called Beauty's patch. It is Black Beauty! It really *is!* Do you remember me? Young Joe who nearly killed you?"

I was so glad to see him! I've never seen a man so happy, either.

I've been here now for a year.
Joe is always gentle, Claire and
Elspeth are kind, and my work
is easy. All my strength has come
back and I've never been happier.

The sisters have promised never
to sell me. Finally I've found my
home, for ever and ever.

Anna Sewell, who lived from 1820-1878, adored horses. She suffered from a bone disease and, after spraining her ankle as a young girl, she became increasingly lame. For the last six years of her life she couldn't move from her house. She longed to make people more caring about horses, so she wrote "Black Beauty" (her only book), lying on her sofa. Anna died just after it was published, never knowing its success.

Series editor: Lesley Sims
Designed by Katarina Dragoslavic
Cover design by Russell Punter

First published in 2005 by Usborne Publishing Ltd., Usborne House, 83-85 Saffron Hill, London EC1N 8RT, England. www.usborne.com
Copyright © 2005 Usborne Publishing Ltd.
Printed in China. UE. First published in America in 2006.